Penny Dreadful
and the CATastrophe
page 95

Penny Dreadful's
Top 5 Tips for Survival
page 134

Meet Penny Dreadful and her Resigned Relations

Penny
(It's never really her fault…)

Georgia May Morton-Jones
(Penny's genius cousin)

Cosmo
(Penny's best friend)

Daisy
(Penny's annoying sister)

Penny's long-suffering **mom** and **dad**

Very prim-and-proper **Aunt Deedee**

Barry
(Meow, I'm Gran's cat)

Gran
(Normally found fast asleep somewhere)

Penny Dreadful

is a Complete CATastrophe

JFM MHASOND/15 00113/12
Printed and bound by
CPI Group (UK) Ltd, Croydon, CR0 4YY

By **Joanna Nadin**
Illustrated by **Jess Mikhail**

USBORNE

Contents

selection

PIECE OF MOON $200

Penny
Dreadful
and the
Rat

My name is not actually Penny Dreadful. It is Penelope Jones.

The "Dreadful" part is my dad's **JOKE**. I know it is a joke because every time he says it he laughs like a honking goose. But I do not see the funny side.

Plus it is not even true that I am dreadful. It is like Gran says, i.e. that I am a **MAGNET FOR DISASTER**. Mom says if Gran kept a better eye on me in the first place instead of on Chuck Hernandez, soap opera superstar, then I might not be quite so magnetic. But Gran says if Mom wasn't so busy answering phones for Dr. Cement, who is her boss and who has bulgy eyes like hard-boiled eggs (which is why everyone calls him Dr. Bugeye), and Dad wasn't so busy solving crises at the city council, then they would be able to solve some crises at 73 Rollins Road, i.e. our house. So you see it is completely not my fault.

★ ☆ ★ ★

For instance, the **DISASTER** with Rooney, who is our class rat, might not have even been such a **DISASTER** if it wasn't for several **OTHER** people, i.e.:

1. Georgia May Morton-Jones,

who is my cousin, and who should **NOT** have brought over her real leather briefcase with two compartments and a secret slot.

b. Lilya Bobylev, who is Georgia May Morton-Jones's nanny, and who should have taken an aspirin after all.

3. Cosmo Moon Webster, who is my best friend (even though he is a boy and exactly a week older than me), and who should not have made the **AMAZING MAZE**.

iv) Dad, who is my dad, who should not have claimed he was a **RESPONSIBLE ADULT**, because as Mom says, he is **CLEARLY NOT**.

e. Miss Patterson, who is our class teacher and very tall and thin like a beanpole, and who should have gotten a guinea pig after all.

But it **WAS** a **DISASTER**, and this is why…

✭ ✩ ✯ ✦

What happens is that Mr. Schumann, who is our principal, and who is mostly saying things like "Penelope Jones, for the umpteenth time will you please sit with your bottom on the chair and your feet on the floor and **NOT** the other way around," says something different, i.e. that our class is allowed a pet, and we will all take turns taking care of it on weekends, and it will teach us about

RESPONSIBILITY,

and a guinea pig would be a good idea.

Only then Miss Patterson decides that the
pet should teach us about **TOLERANCE**
as well, i.e. we should get an animal that is

UNPOPULAR FOR NO GOOD REASON. So then
everyone starts to have **BRILLIANT IDEAS™**
about what pet to get, e.g. Luke Bruce thinks
we should get a shark and Cosmo thinks we

 should get a
Tyrannosaurus
rex. Only Miss
Patterson
says **a)**
we cannot
fit a shark
into the
classroom,

and **b)** Tyrannosauruses
are **EXTINCT** and **DEAD**.

So Bridget Grimes,
who is the star student
and Mr. Schumann's
favorite, says we should
get a rat, because they

are actually **CLEAN** and **SMART** (i.e. like her)
and Miss Patterson agrees and the next day
there is a rat in a glass tank where the locusts
used to be (which is another story entirely).
And then Miss Patterson says we can each
put a name in a hat (only it is not a hat,
it is an old paint jar), and she will pull one out
and that is what we will call him, and it has to
be a boy's name because it is a boy rat, so no
*Princess*es please. So I put in *Ichabod* (which is

what my dad wanted to call
me only Mom said no
because it is too weird
and also I am not a
boy), and Cosmo
puts in *Flame*.

Only Miss Patterson does not pull those names
out she pulls out

ROONEY

which was Henry Potts's idea. So Cosmo gets
angry because Henry Potts is his mortal enemy
and he throws an eraser at him, and Henry
throws a pencil case back and it hits Rooney's
glass tank and Rooney squeaks, and they both
get sent to Mr. Schumann.

✶ ✩ ✶ ✦

Mr. Schumann says their punishment is that they are **DISQUALIFIED** from taking care of Rooney until they can learn some **RESPONSIBILITY**. Only Cosmo says Rooney is supposed to be teaching them **RESPONSIBILITY**, so if they don't take care of him how can they learn it? And Henry Potts agrees (even though he is a mortal enemy), and also says Mr. Schumann is being **INTOLERANT**. Only Mr. Schumann does not agree and says

they will be disqualified forever if they do not
PIPE DOWN. Which they do, and they decide
that Mr. Schumann is their mortal enemy for the
moment and they will not throw erasers at each
other for at least an hour or so.

★ ★ ★ ★

So then
Miss Patterson
makes the rest
of us write our
own names
on pieces of
paper and put
those into the
hat that is
not a hat,

and she will pull one name out and that is who
will get Rooney for the first weekend, and
unbelievably it is **MY NAME**, i.e. Penelope Jones.
And I can tell Bridget Grimes is not pleased
about this, and nor is Miss
Patterson, only she says maybe
the **RESPONSIBILITY** will
do me good.

And I think maybe **TOLERANCE** will do her good, but I do not say it because I do not want to get sent to Mr. Schumann and be **DISQUALIFIED**.

★ ☆ ✭ ✦

Only when I get home on Friday with Rooney in the glass tank it is clear that Mom is not pleased either, because she says she is up to **HERE** with Barry (who is Gran's cat, and who has eaten the last of the cheese again, even though Mom has told Gran it is **CAT FOOD AND CAT FOOD ONLY**), and Daisy (who is my sister, and is very irritating, and who says she will die if she doesn't get a pony like Lucy B. Finnegan), and so the last thing she needs is more animal hoo-ha, especially with a filthy rat. So I tell her he is not filthy, he is in fact **CLEAN** and **SMART**,

and amazingly
Dad agrees
and he helps
me set up a
special maze for
Rooney with toilet-
paper rolls and
some cat food in
the middle, and
Rooney solves it
in thirty-three
seconds, which is
faster than Barry
(who just eats a
raisin he finds
on the floor).

And everyone agrees Rooney is a wonderful pet
and **COMPLETELY CLEVER**, although Daisy
says a pony would be **CLEANER** because ponies
do not poop on your hand, which is true. And
then I say it is time to put Rooney
away because it is not just
about **TOLERANCE** it is
about **RESPONSIBILITY**.

✦ ✧ ✦ ✦

And I prove I am utterly responsible because I do not let Rooney sleep in my bed that night, or investigate outside the window in the morning, or make friends with Barry, even though I have seen it on *Animal SOS* (which is a TV program where animals are always almost dying but then they don't and it is **MIRACULOUS**), because Gran says Barry is not tolerant of anyone (e.g. the man who does the news), and so he is not likely to be friends with a rat, plus Barry is an extraordinary hunter and will pounce on Rooney and murder him. So I responsibly keep Rooney in his glass tank in my bedroom and I feed him my cereal through the wire on the top, which is what we are doing when the doorbell rings.

It is my cousin Georgia May Morton-Jones,

with her nanny, Lilya Bobylev, who asks Mom

if she can watch Georgia May because she

has to see Dr. Cement about her earache.

Aunt Deedee, who is Georgia May's mom

and is usually shouting on the phone with the

NEW YORK OFFICE, says pain is all in the mind and that when she broke her arm she only took an aspirin and did three conference calls and fired Miss Fazakerley-Knowles before she went to the hospital. Only Lilya says the pain is not all in her mind it is all in her ear. But Mom says she can't watch Georgia May because she has to see Dr. Cement, only not for an earache, but for filing, and Gran is not allowed to watch Georgia May except in **END OF THE WORLD EMERGENCIES** because of the time Georgia May shaved all her hair off. So Dad says **HE** will watch her, because he is a **RESPONSIBLE ADULT** and anyway, how hard can it be? And I can tell Mom is about to say something about that, and possibly so is Georgia May, but then the phone rings and it is Lucy B. Finnegan asking if Daisy can come horse riding, so then Mom has to find Daisy's riding boots and drop her off at the stables on the way to Dr. Cement's so it is agreed that Dad will be in charge.

Normally I am completely **GLOOMY** when Georgia May comes to play because she is only four, and not at all interested in my

in case they ruin her clothes or her fingers (which are very important because Mr. Nakamura says she shows potential on the violin). Only this time I have Rooney, and Georgia May is really excited because she has learned lots of interesting rat facts in biological science at The Greely Academy

for Girls,

e.g. that

rats see

with their

whiskers

and keep cool

with their tails.

We do not have biological science at St. Regina's, we have nature walks (only not at the moment because Miss Patterson says she is not taking anyone into Hooton Hollow again until I can be trusted not to fall out of a tree). Anyway, we are about to test if Rooney can see with his whiskers, when it turns out that Mom was wrong because Dad is suddenly **VERY RESPONSIBLE** and says we are not allowed to let Rooney wander around the floor, in case of **UNFORESEEN CIRCUMSTANCES**, e.g. Barry. Only Georgia May says they are not **UNFORESEEN** because he has just **FORESEEN** them, but Dad says he is not getting into an argument about words, because in fact he could have

been a professor if he hadn't married Mom.
But Georgia May says no he could not,
because he does not have a real leather
briefcase, he has a pink backpack with a
picture of a princess on it (which in fact he
borrowed from Daisy because Barry chewed
his black one). And Dad says it is not
essential to have a real leather briefcase to be
a professor and Georgia May says yes it is,
which is why Aunt Deedee bought her one
yesterday, and she shows it to him, and it is
very definitely real leather, plus it has two
compartments and a secret slot. Which is
when I have my

BRILLIANT IDEA™

which is to turn
her briefcase into
a portable rat
carrier, and we
can put Rooney
in the secret slot
and his food in
one of the
compartments
and his bed in
the other.

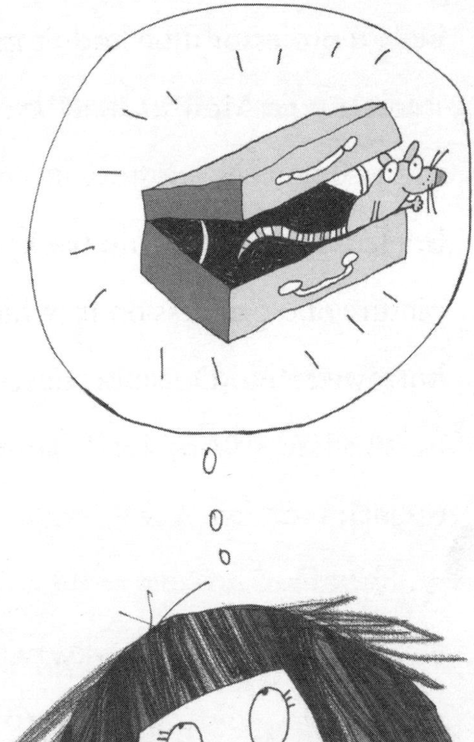

Only Georgia May Morton-Jones does not think this is so **BRILLIANT** because Rooney will poop on the leather, and Dad looks like he possibly agrees, only the doorbell rings again so he has to answer it. And this time it is Cosmo Moon Webster, who has come to be **RESPONSIBLE** and **TOLERANT** with Rooney too.

Then Dad has one of his

BRIGHT IDEAS™

(which are like **BRILLIANT** ones, only Mom almost never thinks they are **BRIGHT** or **BRILLIANT**), which is to make pizza for everyone for lunch. Only we don't have any cheese, because Barry has eaten it, so Dad says he will go to the store and Gran can be in charge and it will only be for an hour and Aunt Deedee will never know.

★ ☆ ✱ ✦

So for a while we are totally responsible, i.e. we watch *Animal SOS* with Gran (only Georgia May keeps her eyes shut because there is a monkey who miraculously **DOES NOT DIE** even though another monkey has bitten his arm and it is hanging off, and also because she is only allowed to watch the Math Channel). But then Cosmo notices that Gran is fast asleep and says maybe it would be **RESPONSIBLE** to go upstairs and do something quiet, e.g. make Rooney a new and **IMPROVED** maze.

And we do, and it is an **AMAZING** maze, because you start on the Pirate's Ship (which is actually a shoebox with some sails),

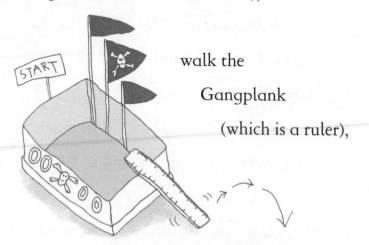

walk the
Gangplank
(which is a ruler),

dive into the Shark-Infested
Waters (which is actually
an old cookie tin with some

plastic animals in it), then go through the
Catacombs of Death (which is fourteen toilet-
paper rolls joined up in a tube),

and into the Haunted
House (which is Daisy's
dollhouse), up the
mini stairs, out the
mini bathroom window

and into the Prize Arena
(which is the glass tank), where there
is a chocolate cookie for a prize (because
for once Barry has eaten all the cat food).

And Rooney is obviously as smart as a professor
even without a real leather briefcase, because
he goes along the Gangplank, into the
Shark-Infested Waters – where
he actually attacks
a hammerhead
(i.e. a plastic sheep)
– then goes into the
Catacombs of Death.
Only the catacombs
fall apart because
Cosmo has stepped on them accidentally, and so I
help Rooney a little by putting him through the
front door of the Haunted House.

And **THAT** is where the **DISASTER** begins,
i.e. Rooney does not come out of the bathroom

window. In fact he does not come out **AT ALL**.
So Cosmo says he has probably just decided to
take a nap in the genuine oak miniature
four-poster bed with lace canopy. Only then
ten minutes have gone and he is still not awake,
and when we open up the front of the house the
genuine oak miniature four-poster bed only has
three posters left, and there is a big hole in the
wall, and Rooney is nowhere to be seen,
i.e. he is not in the
Catacombs
of Death, or
in the Pirate
Ship, or
even in my
bedroom.

So then Cosmo says maybe we should use Barry to sniff Rooney out, only we will capture Rooney with an ice-cream tub before Barry pounces and murders him. Only Barry is not too interested in getting up from the sofa because he is watching a program about bees, so Cosmo gives him the chocolate cookie prize and he is suddenly more interested.

And he does some sniffing
in my room and he finds
a lot of things, e.g.:

a) An old sock

2. A piece of licorice

c. A dead fly

But **NO ROONEY**. Cosmo says he has probably
fled to his freedom, which is a **GOOD THING**,
because Cosmo's mom (who is called Sunflower,
even though her real name is Barbara) does not
believe in keeping animals locked in cages

because it is **AGAINST THEIR RIGHTS**. But I do not think this is a **GOOD THING** and nor will Miss Patterson and so I am suddenly very gloomy, which is when Dad gets back with the cheese and says, "Why the long face, Jones?"

And so I tell him, and amazingly instead of telling me I am **IRRESPONSIBLE**, he says,

"He'll be in the plumbing. Rats always are."

And he gets a wrench and a pair of pliers,

and says,

> Did I ever tell you I could have
> been a plumber if I hadn't
> met your mother?

Only I do not think this is true because he

unscrews a piece of pipe and water bursts all

over everyone, which is when Mom and

Daisy and Lilya Bobylev

all walk in.

And then it is **MAYHEM**
because Georgia May
Morton-Jones is crying like
CRAZY because she says she will
catch a cold and will miss her violin exam and
Mr. Nakamura will be disappointed in her, and

Lilya Bobylev is crying like
CRAZY because Aunt
Deedee will fire her for
making Mr. Nakamura
disappointed in Georgia
May, and Daisy is crying like
CRAZY because the water has
flooded her chewed-up dollhouse. And she says,

It is **ALL YOUR FAULT**,
Penelope Jones.

42

Only Mom (who has turned slightly palish and her lips are very thin) says it is not my fault, it is **DAD'S**, and he has proved that he is **NOT** a **RESPONSIBLE ADULT** and that it is the last time she is **EVER** leaving him in charge.

But even though she says it is not my fault I am still completely gloomy because I do not think Bridget Grimes or Miss Patterson or Mr. Schumann will agree when I go to school on Monday with no Rooney.

But then Dad has another of his

BRIGHT IDEAS™,

which is to go to Paradise Pets and buy a new rat that looks just like Rooney and **NO ONE WILL BE ANY THE WISER**. And Mom says this is really **NOT BRIGHT** because we are bound to get found out, only Dad does not agree and Mom says "Fine" because she has to figure out the pipes and Daisy's dollhouse and some dry clothes for Georgia May Morton-Jones.

And so that is what we do. We buy a new rat named Rooney 2 and he looks just the same and so Dad is right – **NO ONE WILL BE ANY THE WISER**.

★ ☆ ✦ ✸

Especially not Miss Patterson, who is completely pleased when I come in on Monday with the glass tank and Rooney 2 inside it, and she says I have "proved my critics wrong," i.e. Bridget Grimes.

Only Bridget Grimes does not like being proved

wrong, and in history, when we are supposed to

be learning about King Alfred, who burned some

cakes, she is staring very hard at Rooney and says,

Miss Patterson, why is Rooney so
fat? I think Penelope Jones has been
feeding him irresponsible things and
he is obese and will die.

Only for once Miss Patterson does not agree and reminds her about **INTOLERANCE** and makes her go and sit in the corner with Alexander Pringle, who is in trouble for eating peanut butter sandwiches in class again.

✷ ✸ ✷ ✸

And so I am just thinking that **DISASTER** has been **AVERTED** when it gets **VERTED** again, i.e. on Wednesday morning we go into class and Rooney has had eight rat babies. And I say it is a **MIRACLE** because Rooney is a boy.

Only Miss Patterson does not agree that it is **MIRACULOUS** and she sends me to Mr. Schumann, where I have to explain about the maze, and the pipes, and Rooney 2. But, like I tell him, it is not my fault, it is just that I am a **MAGNET FOR DISASTER**. Only Mr. Schumann does not agree and I am banned from learning about **RESPONSIBILITY** for the rest of the year, and so is anyone else until he can figure out what to do with all the rat babies. So everyone else starts being very **INTOLERANT** because they do not get to look after Rooney 2 at all and Henry Potts says I have **IRRESPONSIBLY** lost Rooney 1, who has probably been eaten by **INTOLERANT** wolves or jaguars. And Cosmo says jaguars do not eat rats they eat boys named Potts, and then Henry Potts says he is being **INTOLERANT**, and Cosmo says Henry is being **INTOLERANT** and then Miss Patterson tells everyone to stop the **INTOLERANCE NONSENSE** and open up their art books.

✦ ✦ ✦ ✦

Only when I get home, I find out that I have not lost Rooney 1 and he has not been eaten by jaguars or wolves, he is back at Paradise Pets. What happened was he had been **ASLEEP** in the secret slot in Georgia May Morton-Jones's real leather briefcase. Only he woke up during her violin exam and bit Mr. Nakamura, who was very **INTOLERANT** and failed Georgia May. And I know this because Aunt Deedee calls Mom to shout about the filthy rat.

But Mom tells Aunt Deedee that in fact rats are not filthy, they are **CLEAN** and **SMART**, and she should be more **TOLERANT**.

But Aunt Deedee says there is such a thing as **TOO MUCH TOLERANCE**, which is why Georgia May is on Grade 4 violin and I can't even play "Twinkle Twinkle Little Star" on the recorder without getting several notes wrong.

So then Mom says something **INTOLERANT**

and **IRRESPONSIBLE** and Aunt Deedee hangs

up the phone.

And I say in fact it is good that Mom

thinks rats are **CLEAN** and **SMART**,

because Mr. Schumann has actually had a

BRILLIANT IDEA™, which is that we can

take a rat baby home to take care of, but

only if we get **PERMISSION IN WRITING**. Only

Mom says she is up to here with rat nonsense,

and even if they could use the toilet and wash

their hands she is not giving

me **PERMISSION**

IN WRITING to

have a rat baby.

Daisy says, "It is all your fault, Penelope Jones, you are such a complete moron." But it is not my fault. It is just that I am a

Magnet
for
Disaster.

Only now I think about it, maybe it is all Aunt Deedee's fault. Because she is the one who bought the real leather briefcase in the first place.

Penny Dreadful's
Show-and-Tell

There are absolutely lots of people in my class

that are completely and very **ANNOYING**, e.g.

1. Henry Potts, who is always throwing things like erasers and rulers.

2. Brady O'Grady, who is also always throwing things like erasers and rulers and sometimes Henry Potts.

3. Alexander Pringle, who is mostly eating sandwiches when he should not be eating sandwiches.

4. Luke Bruce, who is often putting things up his nose, e.g. a baked bean and a barrette and once a plastic dolphin (but it got stuck and he had to go to Mr. Schumann to get it pulled out with some pliers).

★ ☆ ✦ ✶

But the **BIGGEST ANNOYER** is Bridget Grimes, who is the star student in the class and Mr. Schumann's favorite and is utterly a big show-off, e.g. she has hair that

is down to her waist and she is always swishing it and saying, "My hair is down to my waist, Penelope Jones, and your hair is tangled with glue in it," which is true but is definitely showing off.

Anyway, she is showing off doubly this week because she has a piece of the moon in a glass box and it cost $200 and she has brought it in for show-and-tell and everyone goes "oooh" and "ahh," and Miss Patterson, who is our teacher, and who is tall and thin like a beanpole, says it is the most exciting show-and-tell **EVER** and sends her to see Mr. Schumann for **ANOTHER** gold star, even though she has already gotten five gold stars for her show-and-tell objects, which were:

a. A Roman coin

2. A piece of amber with a dead fly trapped in it

3. A hummingbird moth chrysalis

4. A stamp of Queen Victoria

e) Her penfriend Inka, who is from Finland

I have **NO** gold stars, even though today I have brought in a chocolate chip cookie that had no chocolate chips in it even though it came out of a chocolate chip cookie box, and before that:

1. A dead wasp

b) A bent coin

3. Magic beans, which Miss Patterson said were not magic they were just string beans, only I said how did she know, so we planted them, and it turned out Miss Patterson was wrong because they were not string beans, but also I was wrong because they were French beans, which are not magic, just foreign.

iv) Barry, who is Gran's cat, and who mostly does **NOT** eat cat food, and who ran up the curtain in the cafeteria and got stuck, and the fire department had to come and rescue him and we all got to go on the fire truck (so if you think about it I should get a gold star just for that).

Which I say to Mom when I get home, and I also say, "Please can I have a piece of the moon in a glass box, it is only $200." Only she says no because I have still not paid her back from the time I accidentally called India, **OR** for the hole in the carpet where I tried to invent stain remover, **OR** for the time Rooney chewed a hole in Daisy's dollhouse — and anyway show-and-tell is not about **EXPENSIVE** objects, it is about **INTERESTING** ones or ones you have made **ALL ALONE AND BY YOURSELF**. And I am just about to promise to save up $200 by doing the laundry for instance,

when the doorbell rings and
it is Cosmo Moon Webster,
who says he has come
to cheer me up about
show-and-tell and I say
it is **IMPOSSIBLE** because
I am completely **GLOOMY**.
But Cosmo says I should
be **HAPPY** that I am
not him, as he brought
in an empty glass
jar because his mom
Sunflower (who is
actually named Barbara),
said it symbolizes **SPACE**,
only Miss Patterson did not

get the **SYMBOL** and nor did Bridget Grimes,
who said it is not **SPACE** unless he got the jar out
of a rocket, which he did not, he just got it out of
the pantry.

And I say it is true because my cookie was
more **INTERESTING** than the empty jar, but it
did not get a gold star and I absolutely want one
to beat Bridget Grimes, who is a show-off.
So Cosmo says what we need is a **BRAINSTORM**,
which is where we think up tons of

BRILLIANT IDEAS™

and we choose the best one and that one will
be the most **INTERESTING** show-and-tell
object **EVER**.

★ ☆ ★ ★

So what happens is we do a list and on it are:

a) An alien

b) A dinosaur

3. Buried treasure

d. Queen Victoria

v. A magic amulet

6. A four-leaf clover

7. A tiger

h. The moon (i.e. the **WHOLE** moon,

and not just a piece of it in a glass box)

Which is when we decide we have done
enough brainstorming. And then I say maybe
we should cross off the moon, because we
haven't got a rocket or a pulley to get it back.
And Cosmo says we should also probably cross
off an alien too, if we cannot get to the moon,
and maybe the magic amulet, and the tiger,
and Queen Victoria, and the dinosaur. Which
means we have only got the four-leaf clover
and buried treasure ideas left for our most
INTERESTING object **EVER**. So I say we
should definitely get a four-leaf clover
because then it will also bring us
LUCK to win a gold star as well
as being **INTERESTING**, and
Cosmo agrees.

So we go **SUPER QUICKLY** to the backyard
with a magnifying glass, and some cookies
to keep us **SUSTAINED** on our **ARDUOUS**
JOURNEY (because Cosmo is very big on
ARDUOUS JOURNEYS, and cookies), only when
we get outside there has been a **COMPLETE**
DISASTER because Dad has mown the lawn,
i.e. there is no clover left (and no grass in places
either, because the lawnmower is a little tricky
and Dad is not very good with machines),

which is not **LUCKY** at all. So then we decide to
do Plan B, which is **BURIED TREASURE**, and
we will do it in the daffodil patch, because
Barry poops in the other places in the yard and
I do not think Miss Patterson will give me a
gold star for cat poop.

So we get my garden shovel, which is red and is cracked from where I tried to dig through a rock, and also a spatula from the kitchen drawer, because Daisy says we cannot borrow her shovel because it is has a see-through handle with plastic fish in it, which means it is special and for **SAND ONLY** and I am bound to ruin it because I am a **COMPLETE MORON**. And then

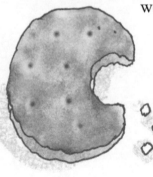 we eat our cookies, because it has been an **ARDUOUS JOURNEY** going to the garage and the kitchen and especially to Daisy's room, because she is doubly irritating today as her friend Lucy B. Finnegan is here and they are pretending to be gymnasts.

FINALLY we start digging for buried treasure

and we find some very interesting things, i.e.:

1. A rusty badge from the museum

b) A broken plate

3. A key

4. Quite a lot of daffodil bulbs

5. Another bent coin

But Cosmo says mostly these are **NOT** interesting things except for the key which is **MYSTERIOUS** and definitely **BURIED TREASURE**, so we show it to Mom. Only she says there is nothing **MYSTERIOUS** about it, it is the back door key that Dad **BURIED** in case we were locked out, only he forgot where he buried it so when we **DID** get locked out (which was not really my fault, I just wanted to see if the key fit through the crack in the sidewalk), we had to break in with a golf club and a hammer. **PLUS** she is not in any way pleased about the daffodil bulbs, which she says need burying again **IMMEDIATELY**.

Which we do, only when we are doing the burying
Cosmo stabs something metal with his spatula
and he says, "Ahoy, *it is buried treasure*, me
hearties," even though we are not being pirates
we are being **ARCHEOLOGISTS**. Plus it turns out
it is not buried treasure either,
it is a water pipe and water starts spurting
everywhere and I say it is **LUCKY** because Mom
has always wanted a water feature, only it turns

out that Mom does not want a water feature
that spurts in through the kitchen window.

Plus now she is **TRIPLY** not pleased because
the pipes have only just been fixed after
Dad unscrewed them to find Rooney the
class rat.

So **THEN** Gran says she has a **BRILLIANT** and **ARCHEOLOGICAL IDEA**, which is that her friend Arthur Peason down the road, who has no hair, and who is on vacation in Bora Bora, needs his vegetable garden dug up, and we can do it for him, so it will be **INTERESTING** and **USEFUL** and a **SURPRISE** all at once. And I am very big on being **USEFUL** and on **SURPRISES**, only Mom is not so sure about how **USEFUL** it will be and about it being the wrong sort of **SURPRISE**.

Only just then Lucy B. Finnegan does a
cartwheel into an armoire, which is not
USEFUL at all, but really **SURPRISING**,

and Mom has to go upstairs to untangle her
from some coat hangers, so we go to Arthur
Peason's **COMPLETELY QUICKLY**, which is
very **ARDUOUS**, so it is lucky we have more
cookies.

✦ ✦ ✦ ✦

And Gran is right, it is **UTTERLY** surprising at
Arthur's, because we find a **DEAD DINOSAUR**.

What happens is I am digging with my
shovel, and Cosmo is annoying some ants
with his spatula, and so far we have only got
a rusty kazoo and four ant bites, when Mrs.
Butterworth from the general store (who has
a mustache and is always saying "I have got
my beady eye on you") walks past, and her
beady eye is definitely on me, because she says,

Which is possibly true, and there is nothing
Mrs. Butterworth can say to that, so then she
goes to be beady somewhere else. And that is
when I dig something up and it is a **BONE** and
underneath it are more **BONES** and I get very
EXCITED, because not only is it

BURIED TREASURE,

it is also a

DINOSAUR,

which is two of our brainstorm things and possibly **TWO GOLD STARS**. Cosmo says he is not at all sure it is a dinosaur because it is very smallish and also has two heads, but I say **OBVIOUSLY** it is a baby two-headed dinosaur and Cosmo agrees and so we dig it all up and put it in the bucket and take it home.

And I am about to show Mom and Dad the amazing **TWO-HEADED BURIED DINOSAUR TREASURE**, but Mom is too busy saying Dad **MUST NOT** try to fix the broken pipe, he must call **MR. HOSE**, who is the plumber, and Dad is too busy saying that he could have been a plumber if he hadn't met Mom, so there is no need to call **MR. HOSE**. And I do not want to see **MR. HOSE** at all because he is not fond of me ever since I tried to help him fix the shower, so I go to my room with the **TWO-HEADED BURIED DINOSAUR TREASURE** and Cosmo goes home with the spatula (because it is covered in ants and he is going to make an ant farm for show-and-tell, which is an **INTERESTING** object, but not as **INTERESTING** as mine).

✦ ✧ ✦ ✦

And **AMAZINGLY** at school the next day Miss
Patterson agrees, i.e. she says the bones are
possibly not dinosaur bones but they are
INFORMATIVE, which is what show-and-tell
is all about, and that I can take them to Mr.
Schumann and get a gold star, which I am
utterly pleased as punch about. Only then
Cosmo says his ants are also **INFORMATIVE**
and **EXCITING** and he takes the lid off the ant
farm (which is actually
a shoebox), which the
ants think is very
EXCITING and
they decide to
escape.

Only **LUCKILY** I have an idea to capture the ants, which is **ALEXANDER PRINGLE**, who is mostly eating sandwiches in class, only this time it will be a **GOOD THING** because the sandwiches will **LURE** the ants and they will all stick to him and then we can **EXILE** him like Napoleon (who we learned about in history yesterday).

Only Alexander Pringle is not so big on being
EXILED and the ants are not so big on Alexander
Pringle, because his sandwiches are cheese and
not jam, and they are in fact more interested in
Bridget Grimes, because she has brought in a
meringue shaped like the Taj Mahal that
she made **ALL ALONE AND BY HERSELF**.
And what happens is that the ants swarm all
over Bridget and one goes up her nose and she
starts screaming and drops the Taj Mahal and
there is meringue and ants everywhere, which is
when Mr. Schumann comes in.

Mr. Schumann is quite often **SICK AND TIRED** of things, e.g. the time I proved that the most cookies you can eat before you are sick is twenty-three. Or the time I told him Gran was dead, which was why I hadn't done my math homework. And today he is definitely **SICK AND TIRED** and it is because of all the show-and-tell **HOO-HAH**, and so he decides to **BAN** show-and-tell from now on until we can learn to bring in things that are not **ALIVE** or **FULL OF SUGAR**, e.g. a collection of thimbles or a program from a ballet.

Only Miss Patterson says in fact Penelope Jones has brought in something that is not **ALIVE** or **FULL OF SUGAR**. And I say yes, it is dinosaur bones, and Miss Patterson says no, it is not dinosaur bones, and I say yes it is, and Miss Patterson says no it is not, and then Mr. Schumann decides he will be the judge of what is a dinosaur and what isn't and he judges and decides possibly it **IS** a dinosaur and he will send it to the museum to check under the microscope and in the meantime I can definitely have a gold star. And then Mr. Eggs (who is the janitor and who smells like dogs) comes to clean up the meringue and the ants and we do The Great Depression for the rest of the day.

★ ☆ ★ ✦

And I am very **EXCITED** on the way home because of the gold star and the museum and I absolutely burst through the door (even though I have been told not to because once I squashed Barry against the wall and he was not in any way **PLEASED**), and I am about to tell everyone that I am an **ARCHEOLOGIST**, when I see there is a very bald brown man in the room with Mom and Dad and Daisy and Gran and he is looking

not in any way **PLEASED** and neither are they.
And it turns out that the man is Arthur Peason,
who has gotten back from
Bora Bora to find out that
someone has dug up George
and Mildred, who are a
dead rabbit and a dead
guinea pig, and now they
will not **REST IN PEACE**,
and nor will he until
they are
back.

And I say,

It wasn't me.

And Gran says,

I told him that.

Because she is
good at keeping secrets,
especially ones that involve
me. Only it is utterly not a
secret because
Mr. Peason says
Mrs. Butterworth says she
saw me and Cosmo doing
the digging, and everyone
knows she has a beady
eye, and so I say,

Well actually, funnily enough we did not find a dead guinea pig or a dead rabbit, but we did find a dead two-headed baby dinosaur and I got a gold star for it in show-and-tell and it is being investigated at the museum under a microscope right now.

And Daisy says,

You are such a **COMPLETE MORON**, Penelope Jones.

And Dad says "Penny Dreadful" and laughs the honking goose laugh, but I do not see the funny side. And nor does Mom. And nor does Mr. Peason.

★ ☆ ✹ ✦

And nor does Mr. Schumann, who is more **SICK AND TIRED** than **EVER** when he has to call the museum to get George and Mildred back from under the microscope because they cannot **REST IN PEACE** and nor can Arthur Peason, and Mr. Schumann says he will possibly not **REST IN PEACE** either until I am at Broadley Junior High. And I say that is not for three years, four months and twenty-seven days yet. And Mr. Schumann says "Exactly" and that he will have that gold star back, thank you very much, because I have proved yet again that I am utterly a menace. And I say I am not a menace, it is just that I am a

But Mr. Schumann does not agree and says there is definitely no show-and-tell from now on and we can just do Roman history instead.

Which is when I get my next

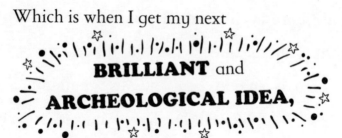

BRILLIANT and

ARCHEOLOGICAL IDEA,

which is to find a Roman fort under our patio.

Only I cannot do it yet because my shovel has

MYSTERIOUSLY disappeared and Cosmo

still has the spatula.

Penny Dreadful

and the

Complete CATastrophe

Our house is usually
completely full of many
people, i.e.:

1. Me, Penelope Jones, who is not
actually dreadful, but just a **MAGNET FOR**

DISASTER.

b. Daisy
Jones, who
is my sister,
and who is
not a menace
either but is very
IRRITATING.

c. Dad, who has to go to a conference on traffic lights, and is very much wishing he was in fact a deep-sea diver (which he says he could be if he hadn't met Mom).

iv) Mom, who says Dad could not be a deep-sea diver because he cannot swim underwater.

5. Barry, who is Gran's cat, and who has eaten two pieces of toast and raspberry jam this morning, even though Mom says it is **CAT FOOD AND CAT FOOD ONLY**.

6 Gran, who gave Barry the toast, because she says it is her birthday and she can **DO WHATEVER SHE LIKES**.

★ ☆ ✦ ✦

Which I do not think is very fair because on my birthday I wanted to **INVENT GOLD** and Mom said **UNDER NO CIRCUMSTANCES** because there is completely too much potential for catastrophe. **BUT** it turns out that Gran cannot **DO WHATEVER SHE LIKES** either, which is mostly eating chocolate cake and watching *Animal SOS* (which is a TV series where animals are always almost dying but then they don't and it is **MIRACULOUS**), because what happens is she accidentally trips over my **PATENTED BURGLAR TRAP** and a bone in her goes snap and the next thing we know she is in the hospital, where there is absolutely no cake at all, just stew and green jello.

I say it is utterly **NOT MY FAULT** because Mom said I was not to put a trap in my bedroom so I did not, I put it in the kitchen, and if you think about it, there is a **POSITIVE SIDE**, i.e. the burglar trap works and if we are ever robbed the thief will go snap and end up in the hospital. But Mom does not see the positive side, because Dad is going to his traffic-light conference and she is going to the hospital to see Gran and there is **NO ONE** to watch me. So I say I will come to the hospital too but Mom says **UNDER NO CIRCUMSTANCES**, and she will just have to see if Lucy B. Finnegan's mom will watch me as well as Daisy. Only Lucy B. Finnegan's mom says she has only just gotten the sticky stuff off the ceiling from last time and so she would rather

not, thank you. And
Mrs. Beasley from two doors
down would also rather not,
and neither would Arthur Peason.

And then the doorbell rings
and Mom says it had
better not be
another thing to
worry about, only it
IS another thing to
worry about, i.e. it is
Cosmo Moon Webster, who is
coming to play for the entire
and whole day because his
mom Sunflower is going on
a yoga retreat.

And that is when Dad has one of his

BRIGHT IDEAS™,

which is that me and Cosmo can go to Aunt

Deedee's house and be looked after by Georgia

May Morton-Jones's nanny, Lilya Bobylev. And

I can tell Mom is not in any way **BIG**
on the ⟨**BRIGHT IDEA™,**⟩ but as Gran is
always saying **BEGGARS CAN'T BE CHOOSERS.**
So Mom puts me and Cosmo **AND** Barry in the
car (because if Barry is left alone he gets stressed
and eats his own tail) and takes us to Aunt
Deedee's house, which is only four roads away
but is very much bigger and also much cleaner
because of all the rules, e.g.:

1. No eating except at the table.

2. No clay or paint or glue
except at the table and only if is
covered in a plastic cloth.

C. No eating clay or paint
or glue.

Plus if you even **LOOK** at a glass candlestick she says, "Do not even think about it, Penelope Jones." And when we get there Lilya Bobylev is also not in any way **BIG** on the *BRIGHT IDEA™,* because of the rules and the glass candlesticks and also Barry, because Aunt Deedee is **NOT A CAT PERSON** because of the fleas. But Mom says Barry does not have fleas (which is possibly a **LIE** because at that **EXACT** moment he is scratching like **CRAZY**), and also that Gran is Georgia May Morton-Jones's gran too and so it is **ONLY FAIR**, and then she drives off **COMPLETELY QUICKLY** before Lilya Bobylev can even **THINK** of an answer.

104

I say,

Do not worry, Lilya Bobylev, I am **UTTERLY RESPONSIBLE** and good at **STICKING TO RULES** and so is Cosmo Moon Webster, and if a flea does jump off Barry we will catch it and kill it with our thumbnail — I have seen it on TV.

And anyway we are utterly **ABANDONED** and practically orphans, so Lilya Bobylev has no choice but to let us in. Only when she does she says there are a lot more rules that we have to **STICK TO**, e.g.:

d. No eating in the garden.

5. No eating the garden.

6. No using purple markers to pretend you have a DISEASE.

(Which is what I did to Georgia May Morton-Jones one time, and she got sent home from The Greely Academy for Girls in case she was **CONTAGIOUS** and Aunt Deedee had to miss a **VITAL DEAL**, which is why she has a new nanny now.)

And Cosmo says, "*Is* '**NO FUN**' *on the list?*" and Lilya checks and says it is not, and Cosmo says he was being **SARCASTIC** but Lilya does not know what that means because she is from Russia (which is where all nannies are from). And then I have my first

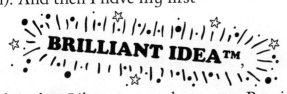

which is that Lilya can teach us some Russian, because Aunt Deedee says it is very useful for business brains (which is why Georgia May is also learning Mandarin). So Lilya agrees and says she will sing a song about a bee and a fox and that we can join in with the chorus. Only it is hard to join in because the words are very fast

and the notes are not at all normalish. And so

when Lilya is singing about the bee or

the fox (I am not sure which), Cosmo has another

BRILLIANT IDEA™, which is to do Russian

dancing, which he saw on TV, as it has lots of

leg-kicking and arm-swooshing and is easier than

words. So me and Cosmo and Georgia

May Morton-Jones do dancing in Russian,

which is when something **UNBELIEVABLE**

happens, which is that I just **LOOK** at a glass

candlestick and it **ACTUALLY** falls off the shelf

and breaks into a gazillion pieces. And I say it

is a **MIRACLE** and Cosmo says it is not a

MIRACLE, it is because I did not just **LOOK**,

I also **SWOOSHED** it with my arm. And Lilya

also says it is not a **MIRACLE**, it is a **MESS**,

and that Georgia May Morton-Jones must
NOT TOUCH THE GLASS because her fingers
are important (because Mr. Nakamura says she
shows potential on the violin) and in fact it would
be a good idea if we watched television instead.

I say we can watch *Animal SOS* and then tell
Gran all about it when she gets home in case
she has missed it in the hospital, because they
don't have cable, they only have romantic novels
and dominoes.

Only Georgia May says she is only allowed to watch the Math Channel, but I say if it is the Math Channel then I am likely to be distracted and possibly may **LOOK** at another candlestick, and Lilya Bobylev thinks this is possibly true, and so we watch *Animal SOS*.

And this week the animal that almost dies but then **MIRACULOUSLY** does not is a Labrador named Hoskins. What happens is that he is in a **TERRIBLE ACCIDENT** with his owner, Mr. Ernest Lemming, and they are both all broken like the candlestick and Mr. Ernest Lemming is in a coma, which is like being asleep but for at least three days (which is longer even than Cosmo, who once slept for fifteen hours, which I said was a record but we checked with Mr. Schumann and it is not). But the vets on *Animal SOS* make Hoskins better by giving him some metal in his leg and a collar like a giant fan and then they take him to see Mr. Ernest Lemming, who is still in the coma, and Mr. Ernest Lemming actually **WAKES UP**.

And the presenter (who is named Griff Hunt) says "That is the power of pets," which is what he says every week, but this week he says it a little bit shoutier. And that is when I have my next **BRILLIANT IDEA™,** which is to take Barry to the hospital to see Gran so she can be revived by the **POWER OF PETS**.

✷ ✶ ✸ ✹

AMAZINGLY Lilya Bobylev says we can go and visit because that way the house will not get broken any more, only we **CANNOT** take Barry but we can take a chocolate cake. Only I do not

think chocolate cake has as much **POWER** and
so Gran will not be as **REVIVED**. And also
Cosmo says that Barry cannot be left alone
because he will eat himself and also what if a
flea jumps off him? So in the end we take him,
but Lilya says he has to go inside a bag with
the chocolate cake, which I do not think is a
good idea because Barry once ate a whole
chocolate cake except for the frosting, which

AMAZINGLY he does

not like.

But I do not say anything because I want to get to the hospital super-quickly to revive Gran. Which we do because Lilya Bobylev gets to drive Aunt Deedee's car, which is "a *hideous gas-guzzling tank*" according to Mom, but "*excellent and enormous*" according to me and Cosmo. And the whole way we are singing the song about the bee and the fox in Russian like **CRAZY**, because by now we have all heard it a lot of times and so even I know some words, which are "*lisa*," which is "fox," and "*pchela*," which is "bee" – or possibly the other way around. But I don't think it matters unless the bee eats the fox, which would be impossible.

The only person who is not singing is Barry and I think it is because he does not know the words, but it turns out it is because he **IS** eating the cake. But luckily he has only eaten the left side, so I scrape off the hair and save the right side and the frosting for Gran, who will not mind because she is always sharing with Barry anyway, plus he is probably very hungry on his **ARDUOUS JOURNEY**. And then Cosmo says he is possibly very hungry too because of the **ARDUOUS JOURNEY** and so am I, so we decide to eat the right side and save the frosting for Gran, which she says is the best part anyway. And by then we are at the hospital.

Only then we realize we have **COMPLETELY**
no idea which floor Gran is on and so Lilya
Bobylev goes to a lady behind a desk who has
glasses that make her look like an owl and
asks for Granny Jones. Only the owl lady
says Granny Jones is not an **ACTUAL**
name and we will have to do
better than that.

Except that Lilya does not know Granny's actual name and nor do I and nor does Cosmo. But Georgia May Morton-Jones says it is Norma Jean, and she goes to The Greely Academy for Girls and so is almost often right, and this time she **IS** right because the owl lady says Norma Jean Jones is on Fothergill Ward, which is on the seventh floor. And Cosmo gets very excited about that because it means there will be an elevator and he is very **BIG** on elevators, especially on getting trapped in one and saving all the mortals who are **PANICKING** and **WAITING TO DIE**. But disappointingly the elevator does not get stuck, although Barry does some panicking (even though he is not a mortal, he is a cat) and starts meowing very loudly.

And then Georgia
May says it is very
OBVIOUS that Barry
is in the bag with the
frosting and we will
be arrested and sent
to prison by the
hospital police. So
then I have my next
BRILLIANT IDEA™
which is to sing the
song about the bee
and the fox in Russian
VERY LOUDLY
and **LOUDER THAN
BARRY**. So we do,

and we are still singing it when we get to Fothergill Ward, where there is **ANOTHER** lady behind a desk, only this one does not look like an owl, this one looks very much like Mrs. Butterworth from the post office, i.e. she has a mustache, and not a beady eye but a beady **EAR**, because she says,

Stop that infernal racket now, this is a hospital not a Talent Show.

Sister Goggins

ROTA

So I do stop, only then Barry is meowing like **CRAZY** and so Cosmo has to pretend he is big on being a cat. And then the beady ear lady tells him to stop **THAT** infernal racket,

so he does and **AMAZINGLY** so does Barry. But it is not because of the beady ear lady it is because he is absolutely **NOT IN THE BAG**.

Which is when Georgia May Morton-Jones starts to cry, which is a **MASSIVE MISTAKE**. Because the beady ear lady says, "What **NOW**?"

And Lilya Bobylev says it is because of Norma Jean Jones, and Georgia May says it is **NOT** because of Norma Jean Jones, it is because we have lost Barry and will be arrested by the hospital police and put in prison. And then the beady ear lady says,

> And who, exactly, is Barry?

And I say,

> He is our uncle.

Which is only **HALF** a lie because Gran says Barry is like a son to her, which would mean he is Dad's brother, i.e. my uncle. And the beady ear lady stops being so beady and cross and says, "Don't worry, he can't have gone far," and she is **RIGHT** because at that **EXACT MOMENT** Barry runs across the floor into a closet and

Georgia May Morton-Jones sobs, "Barry."

Only then the beady ear lady, who is actually

named Sister Goggins and I know that because

it is on a black badge on her uniform, actually

DOES have a beady eye because she sees Barry

and makes a racket which is very **INFERNAL**.

And then **AMAZINGLY** Mom appears and also

makes a racket which is quite infernalish and is

mostly involving, "Penelope Jones, I said

UNDER NO CIRCUMSTANCES were you to

come here because there is

too much potential for

catastrophe," and I say

it is not a catastrophe

and Cosmo says it is

a **CAT**astrophe.

And then everyone is confused for a minute, but not for long because there is a big crash and some more infernal racket and then the **CAT**astrophe, i.e. Barry, who is not in any way pleased, runs out of the closet and towards the sick people, followed by Sister Goggins and Lilya Bobylev and Georgia May Morton-Jones and me and Mom and Cosmo.

And I say it is impressive that he is running **COMPLETELY QUICKLY** because usually he is on the sofa watching television and not even moving a **WHISKER**. Only Sister Goggins is not so **IMPRESSED** because she says he is possibly killing everyone with his cat diseases.

Only when we get to the sick people they are utterly **NOT** killed by cat disease but are **REVIVED**, i.e. Gran says she feels better already just to see Barry and so does Mrs. Bickerstaff, who has a bandaged eye, and so does Mrs. Goldenberg, who has a sore knee. And I say,

THAT IS THE POWER OF PETS.

Only Sister Goggins is not so convinced of the
POWER and puts Barry inside a cardboard
box with holes in it, and tapes the top up just
to be sure.

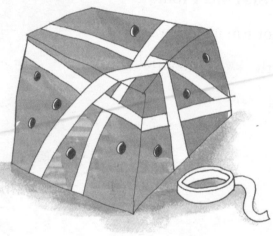

And then Lilya Bobylev says she had better
take Georgia May Morton-Jones home before
Aunt Deedee fires her, and Mom says she had
better take me and Cosmo and Barry home
because I have done enough damage for one day.

And Sister Goggins says she hopes I will be punished, which I do not think is very **SISTERLY** (only I do not say it, not even quietly, because of the beady ear).

And when I get home **I AM** punished and Daisy says I am a **COMPLETE MORON** and Dad does the honking goose laugh. But I do not mind because Gran gets home the next day and says she is completely **REVIVED** and that it is **ALL MY FAULT**, thanks to bringing Barry in the chocolate cake bag. And for once I do not argue.

The End

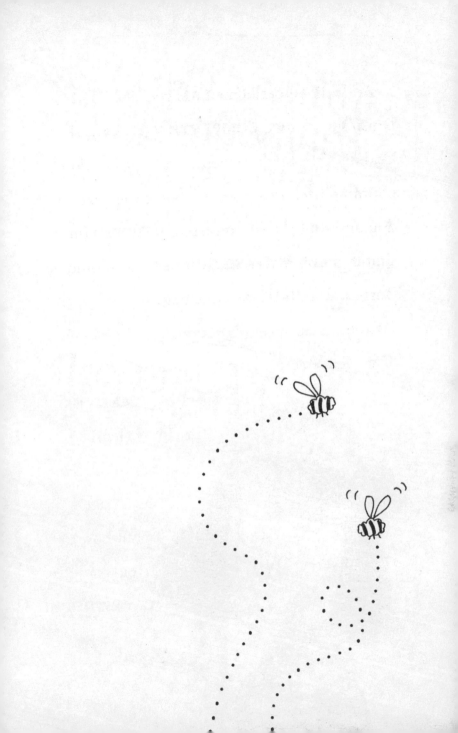

Penny Dreadful's Top **5** Tips for Survival

Sometimes it is very **ARDUOUS** being a

MAGNET FOR DISASTER. Especially if

you are extra specially magnetic, i.e. like me.

But even though it is **ARDUOUS**, it is also

very **INFORMATIVE**,

i.e. I have learned

some important

TOP TIPS

about how to

avoid complete

CATASTROPHE.

Number 1

Get a DISGUISE

It is completely important not to look like me, i.e. Penelope Jones, when I am being very magnetic, e.g. accidentally knocking over a teetering stack of bean cans at the general store. So sometimes I dress up as Cosmo, i.e. in a Jedi outfit and rain boots, because it completely confuses Mrs. Butterworth's beady eye and however hard she **RACKS** her brain she is **DISCOMBOBULATED** as to who to shout at.

Another good disguise is dressing up as a burglar, because burglars wear balaclavas, which **COMPLETELY** cover up their face. Although it is possible you would get shouted at for being a burglar anyway.

Number 2
Collect COLLATERAL, i.e. money

Coins are **EVERYWHERE**, e.g. on the ground outside the general store, down the back of the sofa and mostly in Dad's pants pockets.

Collect them **ALL** because you never know

when you might need them for:

1. Paying people back, e.g. your Aunt Deedee

when you have accidentally broken a glass

vase or called Russia for instance.

b) Buying essential supplies

like cookies or licorice sticks.

iii. Playing ludo, because you have

used the actual plastic counters to

flick at your mortal enemy.

Number 3
Be PREPARED for EVERY EVENTUALITY

DISASTERS are **EVERYWHERE** and you never

know when you might be super-magnetic,

so it is completely important to have a box

of useful things for **EVERY EVENTUALITY,**

i.e. anything, e.g.:

a) COLLATERAL (see above).

2. A DISGUISE (see above).

3. Cookies (for **ARDUOUS**

JOURNEYS).

4. A bottle of dishwashing liquid and a

sponge (for when you have spilled something, or

accidentally drawn some Roman soldiers

marching along the kitchen wall).

e) A flashlight, for when you have

accidentally blown up the vacuum by trying to

suck up the dishwashing liquid, and all the

lights have gone off.

Number 4

Find a TRUSTY SCAPEGOAT

This means someone else to **BLAME**, e.g. in our house everyone mostly blames me, even though it is not usually my fault, it is that I am a **MAGNET FOR DISASTER**. So I usually blame Barry the cat, because he is most often eating things that are **NOT** cat food. E.g. when Daisy said, "Where is my last chocolate-covered cherry, Penelope Jones? I **KNOW** it is you who has eaten it," I said, "But in fact perhaps it is not I, it is **BARRY**, because he completely **ADORES** cherries and chocolate, so ha!"

Number 5

Get a FAITHFUL FRIEND

If you are very magnetic like me, it is

COMPLETELY important to have a faithful

friend, which is not the same thing as a

scapegoat, and is also not the same as a dog

(especially not one that isn't yours but which

you have found outside the general store only it

is not lost at all) but e.g. Cosmo Moon Webster.

Because faithful friends will always stand up

for you, even when you have accidentally

exploded pudding in their microwave,

and even if they are a boy

and exactly a week

older than you.

My
Faithful Friend

Joanna Nadin
wrote this book –
and lots of others
like it. She is small,
funny, clever,
sneaky and musical.
Before she became a writer, she wanted to be a
champion ballroom dancer or a jockey, but she
was actually a lifeguard at a swimming pool,
a radio newsreader, a cleaner in an old people's
home, and a juggler. She likes peanut butter on
toast for breakfast, and jam on toast for dessert.
Her perfect day would involve baking, surfing,
sitting in cafes in Paris, and playing
with her daughter – who reminds
her a lot of Penny Dreadful…

Jess Mikhail

illustrated this book.
She loves creating funny
characters with bright
colors and fancy

patterns to make people smile.
Her favorite place is her tiny home, where she
lives with her tiny dog and spends lots of time
drawing, scanning, scribbling, printing, stamping,
and sometimes using her scary computer. She
loves to rummage through a good charity shop to

find weird and wonderful things. A
perfect day for her would have to
involve a sunny beach and large
amounts of spicy foods and ice
cream (not together).

For Josef and Lily,
who are a little bit Cosmoish,
and totally skill because of it.

First published in the UK in 2011 by Usborne Publishing Ltd., Usborne House,
83-85 Saffron Hill, London EC1N 8RT, England. www.usborne.com

A CIP catalogue record for this book is available from the British Library.

First published in America in 2014 AE.
PB ISBN 9780794530204
ALB ISBN 9781601303400
JFM MJJASOND/15 00113/12
Printed and bound by
CPI Group (UK) Ltd, Croydon, CR0 4YY